M000284594

About the TLS

The *Times Literary Supplement* was born in January 1902. Its first ever front page bashfully stated that 'during the Parliamentary session Literary Supplements to "The Times" will appear as often as may be necessary in order to keep abreast with the more important publications of the day'. Fortunately, the question of necessity was not left in the hands of literary journalists (who, we can imagine, might occasionally push for a holiday or two), and the title became a weekly one. A few years later, the *TLS* split entirely from *The Times*.

Since then, we have prided ourselves on being the world's leading magazine for culture and ideas. Our guiding principle for the selection of pieces remains the same as it ever has been: is it interesting; and is it beautifully written? Over the years, our contributors have included the very best writers and thinkers in the world: from

Virginia Woolf to Seamus Heaney, Sylvia Plath to Susan Sontag, Milan Kundera to Christopher Hitchens, Patricia Highsmith to Martin Scorsese.

The book you are holding is part of a brand-new imprint, TLS Books, by which we are striving to bring more beautiful writing to a wider public. We hope you enjoy it. If you want to read more from us, you'll find a special trial subscription offer to the *TLS* at the back of this book.

In an ever-quickening culture of flipness and facility, fake news and Facebook, the *TLS* is determined to be part of the counter-culture of quality. We believe in expertise, breadth and depth. We believe in the importance of ideas, and the transformative power of art. And we believe that, in reading the *TLS* – in whatever form, be it in a magazine, online or in a book – you are supporting a set of values that we have been proud to uphold for more than a hundred years. So thank you for that.

Stig Abell, 11th Editor of the *TLS*
London, 2020

Sex and the
City of Ladies

Also by Lisa Hilton

Sex and the City of Ladies

*Rewriting history with
Cleopatra, Lucrezia Borgia and
Catherine the Great*

Lisa Hilton

TLS

TLS Books
An imprint of HarperCollins*Publishers*
1 London Bridge Street
London SE1 9GF

The-TLS.co.uk

First published in Great Britain in 2020 by TLS Books

1

A catalogue record for this book is
available from the British Library

ISBN 978-0-00-838960-4

Typeset in Publico Text
Printed and bound in Great Britain by
CPI Group (UK) Ltd, Croydon

MIX
Paper from
responsible sources
FSC™ C007454

This book is produced from independently certified FSC™ paper
to ensure responsible forest management.

For more information, visit: www.harpercollins.co.uk/green

For Sam Ward,
greatest of Catherine's descendants.

Contents

Contents

Sex and the
City of Ladies

ONE

Unexpected Visitors

Here's a list of women:

Livia Drusilla, the wife of a Roman emperor
Eleanor of Aquitaine
Mary Queen of Scots
Catherine de Medici
Roxelana, the wife of Suleiman the
   Magnificent
Empress Cixi of China

Look them up – these women – and before you find out much else about them, you'll be informed that they were poisoners, murderers, adulterers. More often than not, historically renowned women seem to be *bad* women. Because power in women is allied with villainy.

I was thinking about this at my desk in a quiet corner of a Venetian palazzo, surrounded by many books of different kinds, some histories, others biographies or heavily annotated scholarly tracts. Outside, the lagoon was spread thickly with fog, and occasionally I heard a boat's siren sounding across the plain of water. My mind was weary. I had spent the day struggling with these weighty tomes. I lowered my copy of Michel Foucault's *History of Sexuality* and decided to find something more amusing to read.

I chanced on a slight volume bound in faded red cloth among a pile sent from a library. I must have ordered it, though I did not recall doing so. It was *The Book of the City of Ladies*, by Christine de Pisan and, like many other works nowadays, it is said to be written in praise of women. Scarcely had I begun to read when my daughter called me from the kitchen, asking what was for dinner. I put the book to one side, resolving to go back to it the following day.

The next day, I went to the dry cleaner and the supermarket, cleaned the kitchen, did the laundry and swept the courtyard. Finally, seated once more at my desk, I returned to the book. On the first page, Christine asks 'why on earth it was that so many men ... have said and continued to say and write such awful, damning things about women and their ways?' Describing these writers, she continues: 'All seem to speak with one voice and are unanimous in their view that female nature is wholly given up to vice'. Women are routinely accused of being little more than defective men, she says, intellectually and physically inadequate, creeping, whingeing, covetous creatures, who when they are not deceiving their husbands, secretly enjoy being raped. She suggests that the sources of such misogyny are ignorance, spite, envy, fear and impotence. And so Christine resolves to build a city in words, an impregnable fortress in which women 'worthy of praise' will be admitted. Woman may well be lacking in muscular strength, she concedes, but nature has more than compensated her with brains. With her mortar mixed in her inkpot and great swingeing strokes of her pen, Christine sets out to construct a bastion of biographies to show by example that value is predicated on virtue, not gender. The year is 1405.

Christine de Pisan is Europe's earliest known professional female writer. Born in Venice in 1364, she moved to France as a small child, where her father Thomas had received an appointment as physician at the court of Charles V. Married at fifteen, the plague made Christine a widow ten years later, leaving her with an elderly mother and three young children to support. Though women authors were not entirely unknown in the period, Christine, unlike for example Hildegard of Bingen, 260-odd years earlier, did not publish from the security of the cloister. She was a sophisticated, secular woman, enormously well-read and familiar with the most exclusive echelon of French society in a time of impressive cultural development. In a pre-print culture, Christine first found work as a manuscript copyist before beginning to produce her own poetry and tracts. She waded confidently and prominently into one of the primary intellectual debates of the day, siding with Jean Gerson, the Chancellor of the University of Paris, against Pierre Col, the canon of Notre-Dame, on the inadequacies of the bestselling poem *Le Roman de la rose*. Some years before she published *City*, Christine had written *Epistre au Dieu d'amours* (*A Letter to the God of Love*) in which she criticized the author of the *Roman de la rose*, Jean de Meun, for what she considered a despicably silly portrayal of women. In the *City*, Christine expands her argument, pitting herself proudly and wittily against male writers past and present.

I confess, when I picked up *The City of Ladies* I had read more about Christine than I had read by her. She is considered a canonical feminist writer, if not (outside academia) a particularly famous one. *Le Livre de la cité des dames*, as it was first published, was, Simone de Beauvoir noted, 'the first time that we see a woman take up her pen in defence of her sex'. The book takes the form of a series of dialogues between the author and three allegorical figures: Reason, Justice and Rectitude. We meet the author in 1405 as she is in the familiar process of retiring to bed, exhausted after work and childcare. Christine is a character in her own text, an ingénue who innocently repeats the misogynist arguments her reading has thrown up, and she initially portrays herself as despairing over women's lack of virtue. But the allegories wake her, berate her for sloth and set about challenging her on her views about women. They explain that she is ignorant and misinformed by the prejudiced accounts she has read. And they summon a cast of historical characters to reinforce their arguments and recount the exemplary lives of the women who should be the first residents of an allegorical city, where they will be recognized and protected. These include queens of classical history such as Penthesilea and Antiope, numerous female saints and less famous figures, such as a Roman woman who breastfed her own mother in prison. Reason argues – reasonably enough – that negative stereotypes are maintained through women's exclusion from the writing of history; only by examining women's history from a woman's perspective can female virtue be recognized and celebrated. This project Christine undertook. The work was translated into English in 1521, with no new translation attempted until 1982. Within this period, the revolution in women's status sought by Reason took place. Partly.

Nearly every article and commentary I have read on Christine – from the critique of her 'conservative' political theory by Sheila Delany in the 1970s to Tai Shani's 2019 Turner Prize winning installation *DC: Semiramis* – seems nonetheless to see her status as a female author as inherently compromised or problematic. The techniques Christine adopts in *City* include the allegorical 'dream vision', which simultaneously relates and glosses the author's journey. This was a highly typical medieval form, familiar from, say, Dante or Boccaccio. (It is traceable to the fifth-century Roman writer Macrobius's commentary on Cicero's *Dream of Scipio*; and in the sixth century came Boethius's *The Consolations of Philosophy*, which features 'Philosophy' personified as a woman.) Christine also draws on the exemplary biography genre, established in classical antiquity. Or, more specifically, the exemplary female biography, previously attempted by Ovid in *Heroides* and by Chaucer in *The Legend of Good Women*. Both men critiqued misogyny's effect on history, though admittedly in a rather more lackadaisical fashion. But while these writers have been praised more or less uncomplicatedly for their interventions, Christine has been second-guessed, her efforts undercut by a persistent focus on her own place, or role, in the work.

Because her character-self plays the role of Devil's Advocate in the text, upholding the limited views and conventions of the day for Reason, Justice and Rectitude to demolish, Christine has been accused of timidity and hypocrisy, of endorsing the very inequalities (such as fifteenth-century women's lack of legal status), which she professes to challenge. Scholars of both the medieval period and contemporary feminism have seemed particularly troubled by this technique. In her dialogues with Reason, Justice and Rectitude, Christine cites texts that denigrate women, beginning with the *Lamentations* of Matheolus, a thirteenth-century cleric who produced a wordy account of precisely how women make men's lives unbearable (not that anyone would bother with Matheolus nowadays were it not for Christine). She tells Reason about the numerous books she has read which say 'extraordinarily unpleasant things' about women, including a Latin text entitled *On the Secrets of Women*, which claims that the female body is 'flawed' and 'defective'. Reason replies: 'You shouldn't need any other evidence than that of your own body to realize that this book is a complete fabrication and stuffed with lies. Though some may attribute the book to

Aristotle, it is unthinkable that a philosopher as great as he would have produced such outrageous nonsense.'

Even though she voices Reason, Christine has been accused of ambivalence and of disclaiming her authority as a writer – a *female* writer – by hiding behind a fiction. Is she a revolutionary dressed up as a conservative, or the other way around? (No one seems to worry that, in adopting the dream-vision convention, Chaucer was disclaiming his authority as a male writer, peeping out from behind a trope.)

In detecting such covert strategies in *City*, is it not possible that we are falling into precisely the habit demonstrated by Christine's persona, of seeing femaleness as inherently problematic: a defective, untrustworthy version of male authority? *City* is not the work of a timid or anxious author. For a start, it's very funny. Christine's daring is to have her persona come around to meekly accept statements that might seem self evident to a twenty-first-century reader, but which were fairly radical for the fifteenth century – 'it is now clear to me', she says earnestly, 'that God has truly made women's minds sharp enough to learn'. *City* is also audacious. In her reception of the Virtues and her acceptance of their challenge, Christine parallels the sacred words of the Annunciation, when the Virgin Mary received the news that she was to give birth to the Son of God: 'Behold your handmaiden, ready to do your bidding'. There is something of the gleeful relish of early Jane Austen in her brisk dismissal of a thousand years of scholastic certitude: 'Humankind would never have become one with God if Eve hadn't sinned'. But to read Christine anachronistically, to investigate her words for contemporary preoccupations, to judge her a feminist or not, is to miss the point.

Sunk in these thoughts, I slumped against the arm of the chair with my cheek resting on my hand. Outside, it had grown dark. The fog had risen once more, swaddling the palazzo in silence. I must have fallen into a deep sleep, for all of a sudden a beam of light shocked my eyes

11

open. And there between the dining table and the kitchen door, I thought I saw three women. As you can imagine, I was terrified. They had silently entered a room whose doors and windows were all closed. Since I am of the twenty-first century, I didn't imagine that they were apparitions come to tempt me; I thought they were probably crackheads and reached for my mobile phone to call the police. But, as usual, the phone had disappeared among the books and papers. There was nothing for it but to confront them, so I rose to my feet. When I saw that one of them had no head, I sat down again rather quickly.

At least, she didn't so much have no head as many heads. That is, in the place where a person's head is usually found, there was a swirl of images. One moment there was a lazy-eyed, plump-faced blonde, the next a high-cheekboned African woman with plum-dark skin, then a stern, hook-nosed woman with long, painted eyes. On and on they spun. I hesitated, transfixed by infinite variety. When I noticed that one of the faces was Katy Perry's, I realized I was dreaming and relaxed.

'Don't worry', she said. 'You'll get used to it. No one knows what I looked like.'

'I wish I could say the same', put in the second woman, who had a very definite head, generous about the chins, with a large pouffed hat, much beribboned, from which a few curls of thick grey hair poked out. It sat oddly with the rest of her outfit, which was an eighteenth-century military uniform, finished with polished riding boots and spurs.

'So do I', added the third, dressed in a plain grey gown of coarse linen, and with her neck and hair covered by a dark nun's wimple.

'I like your frock. Is it Khaite?' I tried.

'Franciscan.'

A pause.

'There's three of you?' I asked.

'She's catching on', said the woman in military get-up.

'Which one are you?' Even for a person whose sleep had been so abruptly invaded that sounded brusque, so I stood up respectfully and elaborated. 'Reason, Rectitude or Justice?'

'I'm Sophie', she replied. 'But you'll know me as Catherine. This is Lucrezia. And this–'

'I think I know. Cleopatra?'

'Cleopatra the Last, to be precise. There were a few others.'

I held my tongue. There didn't seem much else to do. After a while, the silence felt awkward, so I offered the visitors some tea. When we were all sitting with mismatched mugs – I would have had to root in the cupboard for the best china, then wash it, and besides, excessive domestic competence doesn't play if you want a relatable protagonist – they looked at me expectantly.

'So can we get in?' one of them asked.

I should say that the conversation didn't take place in English. Sometimes they spoke individually, sometimes with one but never the same voice. Between them the women spoke the Egyptian language, Latin, Greek, French, Spanish, German, Italian, Russian and Catalan. Yet we seemed to understand one another.

'It looks like you already have.'

'To the City.'

'Christine's city?'

'Sharp as a knife, this one', said Catherine.

'But – why?' I asked. 'Christine wanted to rescue women whose stories hadn't been told. Everyone knows about you already.'

'Precisely', said Lucrezia. 'It's exhausting, being dragged about, from book to book. We fancy a rest.'

The problem is that Christine had it that 'Only ladies who are of good reputation and worthy of praise will be admitted into this city. To those lacking in virtue, its gates will remain forever closed'. For example: there's the virgin Camilla, who grew up in the wilderness with her father, the deposed king of the Volsci. She trained herself to become a great warrior, won back her father's kingdom and refused to take a husband or sleep with a man. Then there are the Sabine women, who were abducted by the ancient Romans but nonetheless interceded with their vengeful kinsmen to prevent a massacre. Saint

Lucy, Saint Margaret, Saint Justine – all virgins. The three apparitions standing before me were not known for their virtue.

'Ladies', I said, 'I think – probably not.'

'Why not?'

'Well, two of you weren't born when she wrote the book, so–'

'That shouldn't matter. She says the city will stand for all time.'

I took a deep breath. 'Have you ever Googled yourselves? I assume you know what Google is?'

Cleopatra rolled all of her eyes.

'Actually, did you know that I'm a winner in "Epic Historical Rap Battles" on YouTube?' said Catherine.

I did not. Nor did I ask her to clarify.

'You're *wicked*', I explained nervously. 'Any search term you try, you'll find yourselves at the top of the lists: Wicked women, murderous women, notorious women …'

'Perverts', put in Catherine in a satisfied tone.

'I'm sorry, but yes', I said. 'We all know it's not true about the horse. But I have heard the word "abnormal".'

'It's not as though Christine was all that choosy', said Cleopatra. 'She accepted *Medea* into the city, and she didn't even mention me! Not like Chaucer. He said I was "never to her lover truer queen".'

'Only because you topped yourself for love', said Lucrezia, rather insensitively, I thought.

'He made up that pit of snakes! Rubbish.'

Catherine interjected: 'But isn't it all different now everyone's a feminist? We weren't really bad, it was only the patriarchy. We deserve to be re-empowered.'

'I don't think power was really the problem for any of you, if you don't mind my saying.'

'*Em*powerment is different.'

They had a point. Empowerment is a relatively new concept. Worldwide, it inspires and motivates women through quotes and viral hashtags. It sells us T-shirts ('This is what a feminist looks like', 'I Say I'), make-up ('because we're worth it') and scatter cushions with slogans such as 'Empowered women empower women'. It has helped publishing out of a profit slump, with countless variations on the theme of 'Forgotten Kick-ass Feminists of History'.

Christine's *City* was also the product of an interesting historical moment in publishing. It was to be another generation before Johannes Gutenberg adapted the mechanism for move-able type long known in East Asia, to produce the first Western printing press around 1440. Christine was writing on the brink of an infor-mation innovation as profound as the digital revolution that has transformed the modern world. The printing press took books out of the enclosed, Latinate world of the monasteries and made them available in larger numbers to ordinary people, particularly women and girls. Since girls were infrequently educated in Latin, the intellectual lingua franca of Europe, vernac-ular literature was a new and exciting female market. Almost as though in anticipation, Christine wrote *City* in French rather than

Latin. Publishers were tapping into this promising new market and trying to catch their readers young, as we see from an image in the mid-fifteenth-century Harley manuscript entitled 'een groepje lezende vrouwen' ('a little group of reading women'), considered by scholars to be the earliest representation of young girls in a secular classroom. Children's books at the time were designed to imbue religious faith as well as rudimentary literacy, but in this little woodcut we can also detect a significant shift towards the empowerment of women.

More than 600 years later, Western women have never been more empowered, we are told; feminism is no longer a rare and dirty word, and our culture is ready to be remade by and for women as never before. Which is nice.

The rhetoric of empowerment is ubiquitous, but its manifestations fox under scrutiny. Our girls never did come back. In the United States, womb control is regressing from dystopian fiction to legal reality. Christian Dior and many other high fashion brands promote shallow 'couture activism', yet remain reluctant to discuss the huge profits made in states such as Saudi Arabia, where women are welcome to buy a $5,000 jacket but not to try it on in a shop. The abuse of women's rights from Yemen to Mali to India is something to which international politics remains prepared to turn a blind eye. Beyond the facile positivity of a culture that has annexed feminism to commerce, what female power is and what female power does remains conflicted and ambiguous.

'More tea, anyone?' asked Lucrezia.

'No, I'm fine, thanks', I said too quickly.

She giggled.

'I'm sorry, I didn't mean to imply–'

'Poison? We were all at it. Have you seen the Medici archives? Poison for breakfast, lunch and dinner. "A deadly powder mixed with sugar, not unpleasant in taste, which did not immediately drive out the breath of life ... but gradually made its way into the veins and brought death." The Borgia Venom, they called it.'

'But did you really?'

'Never needed to. It's just part of the legend.'

'I did', said Cleopatra, 'on my youngest brother, Ptolemy XIV. One day he was just ... gone.'

'We used to say "travelling in Europe"', added Catherine.

'You're not helping yourselves, ladies.'

'Well, look: we want into the city now. Century after century, they never let up. Victim or villain, we never know whether we're coming or going. It's time we retired from history.'

'I fancy a garden', said Lucrezia, 'somewhere to grow herbs.'

'A nice game of billiards of an evening', said Catherine.

'I'd like my head back', said Cleopatra.

'Forgive me', I said. 'You're feminist icons. Isn't that enough?'

'And a kaftan', added Cleopatra. 'Something comfy.'

* * *

In 1976, the American scholar Laurel Thatcher Ulrich published an article in which she suggested that 'Well-Behaved Women Seldom Make History'. The slogan caught on, becoming a book thirty years later, as well as appearing on a huge variety of merchandise. Ulrich herself expressed discomfort at the phrase's popularity: 'The "well-behaved woman" quote works because it plays into long-standing stereotypes about the invisibility and innate decorum of the female sex ... the problem with this argument is that it not only limits women, it limits history. Good historians are concerned not only with famous people and public events but with broad transformations of human behaviour.'

What do Cleopatra, Lucrezia Borgia and Catherine the Great have in common? Yes, they were women. But suggesting that 'female' is a catch-all category that trumps period, class and acculturation may not be the best perspective from which to practice history. Is it merely anachronistic to seek out and evaluate 'feminism' in classical, medieval or Renaissance writers, or is something more troubling at work? Is it valid to claim that the besmirched reputations of historical female figures are entirely a product of misogyny, in that the women are condemned for 'daring' (a favourite word among today's revisionists) to act in ways that would have been perceived as laudable – or, at least, normal – in their male counter-parts? In attempting to explain away the deeds of powerful women within a 'feminist' narrative of victimhood, are we not being rather crass? Seeing only 'woman', rather than individual, just as Christine objects?

Historical figures have frequently been subsumed by 'black legends', a term coined in the nineteenth century by a biographer of Napoleon to describe the result of a protracted process of distortion, decontextualization or mythologization. Women, especially susceptible to these narrative pressures, must also contend with deep assumptions of cultural femininity. A good example of this is Elizabeth I of England. What was exceptional about Elizabeth was her capacity as a ruler, yet time and time again she is reduced to a bewigged farthingale with a frustrated sex life. Why did she finally execute Mary Queen of Scots? Not because Mary was the figurehead of a terrorist conspiracy that threatened not only Elizabeth's life but also potentially risked England being politically and confessionally subsumed by the imperial ambitions of France and Spain. No, it was because she was jealous: Mary was prettier. Why was Elizabeth's (often frustrating but frequently brilliant) tactic of waiting out political events seen as dithering, rather than strategizing? Because women can't make up their minds.

Like Elizabeth, Cleopatra, Lucrezia and Catherine all lived at points when the power balances of the world were shifting, fissiparous moments when ambition was reshaping governments, economies and the concept of nationhood. Respectively, they saw the emergence of one-man rule in Rome, of Italy as the centre of the Renaissance, and of Russia as a European power. Their power (supreme in the case of

Cleopatra and Catherine) derived in great part from men, but it was not entirely bestowed by them. Their homes – Alexandria, Rome, St Petersburg – were the architectural wonders of their worlds. They belonged to extraordinarily sophisticated societies that were nonetheless brutal; they were highly educated, multilingual slave owners, extravagantly wealthy rulers and patrons who regarded the human sources of that wealth as belonging to another species. Their authority was ordained by God.

(Cleopatra: 'I *was* a god, actually'.)

The classicist Mary Beard has observed that 'We have no template for what a powerful woman looks like, except that she looks rather like a man'. The differentiator should not be in the second description, but rather in the first. The most important thing about Catherine the Great is not that she was a woman. It is that she was the Empress of All the Russias.

'I don't look like a man, do I?' said Catherine.

'Maybe just a bit', said Lucrezia. 'You know, modern. Fluid.'

'The later portraits did you no favours either, to be honest', added Cleopatra.

'I could never get my hair to behave, after poor Michel passed on. You get that terrible frizz with stoves ...'

'Perhaps if we stick to the facts?' I suggested.

'Age before beauty', Lucrezia smiled.

TWO

Cleopatra the Last
(69 BC–30 BC)

The ancestry from which Cleopatra derived her queenship was unequivocally Greek. On the death of Alexander the Great in 323 BC, one of his generals, Ptolemy I, became Satrap in the recently conquered territory of Egypt and in 304 BC declared himself Pharaoh, establishing a dynasty that ruled what was described as the 'greatest of Hellenistic states'. The governing classes of this vast trading empire spoke Koine Greek, though Cleopatra, the daughter of Ptolemy XII, was unusual in also speaking Egyptian. This has led to speculation that her mother was Egyptian, possibly a concubine, but since there is no hard evidence of the woman's existence, her influence on both Cleopatra's culture and physical appearance can only stray into fiction. Hence Cleopatra's face is as much a product of the historical imagination as is her reputation. The only extant images of her issued in her lifetime are coinportraits, designed to emphasize her authority and dignity. Much like the iconized images of Elizabeth I of England – ruff, white skin, red hair – the portraits were less a physical representation of the ruler herself than a means of state-wide familiarization. For a woman whose beauty beguiled Julius Caesar and Mark Antony, the world's most powerful men, it must be said that the images are less than flattering. The coins, dating from her co-rulership of Egypt with Antony, show the lovers on facing sides; the legitimacy of the queen's power is emphasized by a 'Romanization' of her features. Basically, she looks like Mark Antony in drag. This distortion, political and artistic, has shaped Cleopatra's story ever since.

Rome had been economically and militarily engaged in Egypt for a century before Cleopatra's birth in 69 BC. Egypt had been saved from subjugation by Seleucid forces in 168 BC, a delivery that essentially marked the beginning of Egypt's reduced status as a client territory of the growing empire to the West. Several of Cleopatra's Ptolemaic predecessors had been restored to their thrones by Rome after rebellions, including her father, Ptolemy XII, with whom she is likely to have spent two years exiled in Italy. Ptolemy XII appointed his daughter co-regent shortly before his death in 52 BC, after which Cleopatra, aged seventeen, and her ten-year-old brother Ptolemy XIII were proclaimed joint rulers.

The pair soon confronted various challenges: drought, floods, famine, conflict between Egyptian and Roman factions, and the complexities of their obligations as imperial vassals. For a hungry and oppressed populace, it was easy to believe that the new queen had displeased the gods, while Cleopatra's decision to deport fugitives who sought asylum in Egypt after the assassination of a Roman governor was seen as harsh and disloyal to her own people. Yet to protect both her queenship and her state, Cleopatra was bound to follow Rome's dictates, namely that she aid the Republic on request, obey summonses, and preserve the *maiestas* (greatness) of the Roman people. In 50 BC, two years into the siblings' reign, civil war broke out between the Roman Senate, led by Pompey, and the rebel general Julius Caesar. Quite properly, Cleopatra gave her support to Pompey, who not only represented Roman authority, but who had restored her dynasty to its crown. When Pompey was defeated in 48 BC, Cleopatra was exiled to Palestine. There she raised an army, determined to recover her rights in the kingdom now governed by her brother alone.

Ptolemy, meanwhile, sought to ingratiate himself with the triumphant Caesar through an egregious show of might. When the exiled Pompey arrived in Egypt, he was assassinated at the Pharaoh's command. Far from being delighted, however, Caesar was enraged by such a presumptuous gesture against a Roman commander. Arriving four days after the murder, Caesar summoned Ptolemy. Cleopatra seized the moment, got to the palace before her brother, and had herself smuggled in (there is no evidence that any tightly-wrapped carpets were involved). She was presented to the fifty-two-year-old Roman hero and the first result of their encounter was a pledge of support against Ptolemy.

Reinforcements from Rome arrived the following March and Ptolemy was drowned in battle. Cleopatra was officially restored to the throne, which now also had an heir: her son by Caesar. (To complicate matters, Cleopatra was again co-ruling with a younger brother named Ptolemy). The following year Cleopatra joined Caesar in Rome, where he dedicated a golden statue of her to the temple of Venus Genetrix. A mid-first century BC marble bust in the Vatican may be a copy of this statue, which depicted Cleopatra as the goddess Isis, whose diadem she wears. It looks entirely different from the coin portraits, though any real sense of the queen's features is difficult to apprehend, as the face is missing its nose.

In 44 BC, Caesar was assassinated. Cleopatra returned to Egypt, where her brother conveniently died within a month, leaving her free to proclaim her son Caesarion as Ptolemy XV. With Rome divided between the late Caesar's supporters, Antony and Octavian, and his assassins, Brutus and Cassius, Cleopatra had now to judge where to offer support. She declared for the former, a decision that was vindicated by Antony's success at the Battle of Philippi. According to her client obligations she then obeyed a summons from Antony to meet him at Tarsus.

Their encounter, unlike so many of the myths surrounding Cleopatra, was every bit as dazzling in fact as in legend. Cleopatra, considered semi-divine since birth, arrived by river with the full, flamboyant panoply of a goddess, Isis to Antony's (flatteringly implied) Dionysus. Egypt and her queen needed a new champion, and whether Cleopatra set out pragmatically to seduce Antony, or whether the attraction between the two great rulers was a heady imperative, their affair really did move the earth. Antony departed for Rome the next year to marry Octavian's sister, leaving Cleopatra the mother of twins – the ambitiously named Alexander Helios (Sun) and Cleopatra Selene (Moon), who between them were expected to rule the entire cosmos.

'Roman general. Whirlwind romance. Single mother. Again', sniffed Cleopatra.

For the next three years she governed alone. Antony returned in 37 BC, leaving his wife Octavia in Rome, to present Cleopatra with the looted 200,000-volume library of the kings of Pergamon; she gave him another son, Ptolemy Philadelphus. The years of their subsequent joint rule over the Eastern Roman empire saw the beginning of the propaganda campaign that would do so much to distort perceptions of Cleopatra's legacy. As it became increasingly apparent that even the Roman Empire could not contain the ambitions of both Octavian and

Antony, the former began to attack the reputation of his erstwhile comrade. Cleopatra – Queen of Egypt; a foreign operative no matter the loyalty of the past – was a crucial factor in allowing an essentially civil conflict to be inflated into *bellum externum*.

During her time with Caesar in Rome, Cleopatra had already been considered an embodiment of suspicion and mistrust (albeit a highly glamorous one). Writing with hindsight, Lucan called her 'Egypt's shame'. For Horace, she was 'a fatal monster'. Cicero, who was present in the city at the time of Cleopatra's sojourn, peevishly grumbled at her arrogance and at the non-appearance of a promised gift. (He waited until she was safely back in Alexandria to do so.) To the scholar Stacy Schiff she personified 'the occult, alchemical East', a suspect, alluring exoticism, which both seduced and threatened the Roman order. And, the Egyptologist Toby Wilkinson explains, 'Cleopatra's close identification with Antony made it easy for Octavian to brand her public enemy number one, using her to create a distinction between himself, the true Roman, and Antony, the dissolute traitor'.

In 32 BC Antony played right into this stereotype by publicly repudiating his wife Octavia – and hence her brother – in favour of Cleopatra. Octavia was appointed to meet her husband in Athens, bringing fresh supplies of money and troops. Antony refused to see her, sending word that she should return to Rome, leaving him the reinforcements. It was a precise insult, and a huge political gesture. Octavia did as she was told, continuing to live in Antony's house in Rome and to care for their children, cementing her own reputation as the model Roman matron. In terms of the way in which Cleopatra was perceived, this was the breaking point. Contemporaries concurred that Antony was so wild with passion for Cleopatra that he no longer cared for the consequences of his actions, yet Antony's action was as much a declaration of war as of love. Nonetheless, a decision which was to shape the future of the known world has been reduced to a rivalry between two women, or two contrasting types of femininity – the one virtuous and submissive, the other brazen and ambitious.

Octavian propaganda was ramped up, accusing Cleopatra of drink, drugs, animal worship, sorcery and rampantly ruinous luxury. Concomitantly, Antony was formally stripped of his status and reduced to the rank of *privatus*. Up to this point, as the ruler of a client state, Cleopatra had been within her lawful obligations to support Antony. Now that he was deprived of constitutional authority, declaring for him would place her in overt rebellion against Rome.

The eighteenth-century writer Sarah Fielding, in her fictionalized autobiography of Cleopatra, concurs with the latter's critics that Antony was manipulated into abandoning Octavia: 'For notwithstanding all the appearance of Fondness which I put on', says Cleopatra, 'I had, in plain Truth, no other Value for this great Hero, than as he was the

Means of my Power and the Instrument of my Ambition'.

Arguably, Cleopatra had little choice at this juncture – she could really only throw in her lot with Antony. Perhaps she loved him, perhaps he was serviceable, but wherever the truth lay (and no-one knows), she could certainly expect little protection for herself or her state from Octavian. She chose defiance and threw in her lot with Antony.

The confrontation came in 31 BC. Antony and Cleopatra had sailed for Athens to claim back what they had lost with a fleet of 230 ships. They found themselves blockaded by Octavian's forces. At Actium on September 2, the fleet was routed, with only sixty ships escaping. Antony made for Libya and Cleopatra for Alexandria, where Antony joined her some days later as Octavian's forces began their slow march overland from Syria. Cleopatra sent word that she would renounce the throne in favour of her children if the Romans would spare Egypt. Octavian did not reply.

Nine fraught months later Antony led his troops to the gates of Alexandria and when it became clear that all was lost, he committed suicide. Cleopatra had her lover's almost lifeless body brought to her apartments, where he died at her side. The wildly romantic and dramatic accounts of the following days have obscured what few facts are available. We do know that Cleopatra was permitted to arrange Antony's funeral. It is recorded that she refused to eat, fell ill, recovered and was permitted a meeting with Octavian, who threatened reprisals against her children. The date and exact manner of Cleopatra's own suicide are unknown, but by August 12, 30 BC she was dead, the last ruler of a nation whose civilization had endured for 5,000 years.

'Was that all right?' I asked.

Cleopatra was gazing out of the window into the mist. She didn't reply.

THREE

Lucrezia Borgia (1480–1519)

Byron was so obsessed he stole a lock of her hair from the Ambrosiana library; Victor Hugo wrote a novel about her; Donizetti, an opera; the Sisters of Mercy made her a gothchick ('we don't doubt, we don't take direction/Lucrezia, my reflection, dance the ghost with me ...'); and she gets a name check in *The Godfather*. Lucrezia Borgia's inflammatory legend has not evolved much since one contemporary called her 'the greatest whore that ever was in Rome'. Lucrezia was born into a family whose ambition was matched in many respects only by its corruption, but she deserves a degree of autonomous consideration, beyond the pontificate of her father and the political plotting of her brother Cesare.

Despite its appalling reputation for nepotism, the Renaissance Church was also one of the few meritocratic institutions of the day, and by the time of Lucrezia's birth in 1480 the de Borja family had achieved an impressive ascent from minor-landholding obscurity in fourteenth-century Valencia. Lucrezia's father, duly Italianized as Roderigo Borgia, was the nephew of the Catalan Pope Calixtus III. He was made Archbishop of Valencia in 1492 and bribed and bullied his way to the papal throne as Alexander VI the same year. His only daughter Lucrezia was twelve. Bastardy and simony were not news in papal circles, and like many pontiffs, Alexander attempted to establish a secular dynasty through his four children by his mistress Vannozza dei Cattanei: Lucrezia, Cesare, Juan and Gioffre. The Borgias retained their Catalan identity, language and loyalties, and never lost the sense of themselves as outsiders, spurred to ever-greater magnificence by the contempt in which the Roman nobility held them. The incest rumours that dogged

Lucrezia much of her life sprang – plausibly or not – from this intense early closeness; certainly Pope Alexander had no qualms about having his beloved daughter raised in the home of his cousin Adriana di Mila, who was conveniently the mother-in-law of another mistress, the teenage Giulia Farnese.

In accordance with her father's ambitions, Lucrezia was given a similarly princely education to that received by her brothers – she spoke and wrote five languages, including Latin and Greek, was knowledgeable about humanist scholarship and loved poetry and dancing, at which she excelled. Even allowing for sycophancy, the blonde Lucrezia seems to have been genuinely beautiful: 'her mouth is rather large, the teeth brilliantly white, her neck is slender and fair, the bust admirably proportioned', reported one enthusiastic commentator, and she was schooled early in the art of *bella figura*, never failing to make a suitable display in unimaginably costly dresses and jewels.

At barely thirteen, Lucrezia made the first of a series of dynastic marriages dictated by the men of her family, to Giovanni Sforza of Pesaro, a minor yet strategically placed relative of the powerful Sforzas of Milan. But by 1496 the union was deemed redundant. Sforza bridled that His Holiness wished to take away his wife in order to have her for himself. The Vatican airily declared him impotent, and annulled the marriage on grounds of non-consummation. Despite the fact that Sforza's first wife had died in childbed, the Pope insisted that Lucrezia was still a virgin, which had the ambassadors of Europe falling about.

While there is no definitive proof of the scandalous accusations of incest that have always dogged Lucrezia's reputation, there are certainly curious ambiguities. While waiting for the annulment to be finalized, in the summer of 1497, Lucrezia retired to the convent of San Sisto outside Rome. The separation was legalized in December, and the following February two bodies were found in the river Tiber. Pedro

Calderon, the Pope's personal servant, and Pantalisea, Lucrezia's ladies' maid, had been murdered. In March, the Ferrarese ambassador reported on rumours that the Pope's daughter had given birth to a child. Some speculated that Lucrezia had had an affair with Calderon, assisted by her servant, and that they had been disposed of as punishment. Others claimed that this was a ruse to divert attention from the fact that the child had been fathered by either Cesare Borgia or the Pope himself.

That the child existed was not in doubt. Named Giovanni Borgia, known as the *Infans Romanus*, he was legitimized not once but twice, first with Cesare named as the father, and then in a Papal Bull of 1502, as Alexander's own son. Whoever Giovanni's father really was, there is no proof that Lucrezia was not his mother.

The Italian chronicler Guicciardini was one among the many who commented on the gossip surrounding the papal family: 'there were reports that not only did the brothers commit incest with their sister Lucrezia, but her father as well'. In the same year as Lucrezia's divorce, Juan too was murdered. The culprit was widely believed to be Cesare. Machiavelli, writing later, suggested that both brothers were in love with Lucrezia, and that their rivalry had provoked the crime. Lucrezia and Cesare were indeed devoted to one another throughout their lives, and it may have been that these two gorgeous, ambitious siblings never found anyone else to match the other – Cesare in his youth was described as the most beautiful man in Italy.

Whether or not Lucrezia had sexual relationships with her father and brother, the Borgias certainly believed in keeping things in the family. Gioffre's bride, Sancia of Naples, was also rumoured to be having an affair with Cesare, and now the Pope proposed Alfonso Duke of Bisceglie, Sancia's brother, as Lucrezia's next husband. On theological grounds, this was legally incest, since Lucrezia and Alfonso were within the prohibited 'degrees' set out on marriage to relations as determined by canon law, but as Lucrezia's father was head of the Church, this niggle was swiftly dispensed with.

(Given the general climate of sexual license in Rome at the time, intra-familial relations might well have seemed a prudent option. Syphilis was rife, and Cesare certainly fell victim to it. One supposed cure was to bathe the sores in olive oil, which was then resold for cooking.)

Lucrezia and Alfonso's wedding was celebrated in July 1498, but even as the party went on at the Vatican, papal policy was turning away from Naples towards an alliance with France. Lucrezia quickly became pregnant, but after just six months of marriage, Alfonso fled Rome, warned that he too was about to become a disposable husband. Shortly after, Lucrezia left the Holy City for Spoleto, which she was to govern alone as papal regent. But, in October, while Pope Alexander worked secretly on restructuring his power base, the couple returned to Rome for the baptism of their son Rodrigo. Twenty-eight cardinals celebrated the

Mass, and it seemed that Alfonso was back in favour.

The following July, Alfonso was dragged from his rooms in the Torre de Borgia by Cesare's henchmen and stabbed. Lucrezia apparently fainted when she heard the news, but Alfonso survived the attack, tended by her. Lucrezia's devotion was clearly perceived by her father as insubordination, as a month later poor Alfonso was strangled, and Lucrezia dispatched to Nepi. The Venetian ambassador observed: 'Madonna Lucrezia, who is wise and generous, was formerly in favour with the Pope, but now he no longer loves her'.

While Lucrezia was brought to heel in the provinces, signing her letters from Nepi 'The very Unhappy One', Cesare was inflicting ruthless Borgia justice on anyone who dared to oppose the family in Rome. 'Every day', reported the diarist Sanudo, 'people are found murdered, four or five every night, even bishops, prelates and others ... everyone in Rome is afraid of being murdered.' Alfonso's death did not appear to alter Lucrezia's loyalty to Cesare, and it was he who persuaded her to acquiesce in another marriage scheme (to another Alfonso): the Borgia ambition now soared to an alliance with one of the most prestigious aristocratic dynasties of Italy, the Este dukes of Ferrara. The d'Este family was horrified at the prospect, but honour bowed to pragmatism and in 1501 the marriage contract was signed.

Lucrezia was unable to blot the taint of her past. And incidents such as the notorious 'chestnut banquet', where fifty prostitutes crawled naked between the Vatican's dinner tables in pursuit of roast chestnuts, rather undermined the Ferrarese ambassador's description of Lucrezia as 'extremely graceful in every way ... a most devout and God-fearing Christian'. Nonetheless, she was a success as Duchess of Ferrara, where she lived until her death after childbirth in 1519. Despite a lengthy affair with her brother-in-law, the Marquis of Mantua, her third marriage was, by contemporary standards, a good one, producing seven children. She frequently acted as regent of the duchy, while her account books show that the court continued to flourish, attracting artists of the calibre of Titian, Bellini and Ariosto, who in his epic poem *Orlando Furioso* declared Lucrezia's virtues superior to those of her celebrated Roman namesake.

Lucrezia possessed her share of the Borgia political acuity. While the Este marriage was being negotiated, Pope Alexander was obliged to leave Rome. In an unprecedented gesture, he left the administration of the Vatican in Lucrezia's hands. 'Before His Holiness ... left Rome, he entrusted the palace and all his affairs to his daughter Lucrezia, authorizing her to open all letters addressed to him', marvelled the historian Johann Burchard.

Lucrezia was equally praised by her contemporaries for her governorship of Spoleto and her regencies at Ferrara. Twentieth-century research has illuminated a sincere and profound engagement with religion, which contrasts sharply with her unscrupulous reputation. A document from the 1520s discovered in 1901 describes Lucrezia as having taken the habit of a tertiary Franciscan nun, in which she was to be buried. A series of letters written in 1515 between Lucrezia and the Dominican Tommaso Caiani attests to Lucrezia's deep spiritual commitment, and to an awareness of the anomalies and challenges of her position as the scion of a powerful yet compromised family. In one letter, Lucrezia requests a commentary on Psalm 45, which includes verses such as: 'Kings' daughters were among thy honourable women, upon thy right hand did stand the queen in gold of Ophir'. And: 'Hearken, O daughter, and consider, and incline thine ear; forget also thine own people, and thy father's house'.

After giving birth to her fourth child by Alfonso d'Este, Lucrezia asked for an explanation of the purification of the Virgin Mary, and elsewhere states her desire to *rimanere immacolata dei peccati della lingua'* (to remain unstained by the sins of the tongue). This suggests more than a degree of self-awareness.

In turn, Caiani, who as a strict Dominican was certainly no friend to the Borgias, eulogized her as having surpassed in holiness all other women of the Italian courts.

Lucrezia frequently made retreats at the Clarissan monastery of Corpus Domini, where she also commissioned a book of spiritual exercises for her ladies-in-waiting. In 1510, she funded a new convent for the order in the Terranuova quarter of Ferrara, in which she established twenty-two nuns. Women's spirituality seems to have been of particular interest to her; during her time at Spoleto she requested visits from a particularly holy nun, Sister Colomba di Rieti, and also corresponded with the immured anchorite sisters of the Murate in Florence. Lucrezia's piety was not untypical in a period where every aspect of life was dominated by religion, but the intensity of her curiosity and commitment might suggest a need not only to atone for the sins of her family, but also to establish herself beyond them. She was, then, an individual who used her wealth and position to further the aims of the Church, whose reputation, like her own, her father had so enduringly sullied.

'What happened to Rodrigo?' I asked. 'Your little boy?'

'I had to leave him in Rome. They wouldn't let me take him to Ferrara. He was only two.'

Rodrigo never saw his mother again. He died in Bari at the age of twelve.

FOUR

Catherine the Great (1729–96)

Princess Sophie Friederike Auguste von Anhalt-Zerbst-Dornburg saw nothing worth recording about her childhood in her father's province of the Holy Roman Empire, though it remained one of her charms as Empress that she retained some elements of her earthy German upbringing (including a fondness for darning and an interest in the bowel movements of her loved ones). She was introduced to her future husband, Grand Duke Peter, heir to the Romanov dynasty, in 1739, at the age of ten, and refused to allow the fact that they loathed one another on sight to interfere with her ambitions. Having been singled out as the future bride of the Tsar, her name, religion and native language were as dispensable as her emotions.

Her objectives from the start were popularity with the Russian people and the favour of her husband's aunt, the Grand Duchess (soon to be Empress), Elizabeth.

Catherine, as she was re-baptised in Eastern Orthodoxy, was to benefit from an extraordinary anomaly in the laws of succession that governed inheritance within Europe's royal families. In 1722, her husband's great-grandfather Peter the Great had promulgated a new law under which the ruler of Russia was required to nominate a successor, whether or not that successor was a member of the Romanov dynasty. This was true autocracy, endowing the Russian Tsars with 'a prerogative claimed by no other contemporary monarch'. Remarkably, in the period between the Petrine succession law and the Pauline revocation of it in 1797, which restored male primogeniture, women governed Russia. Equally remarkably, this approximate century saw Russia's emergence as a major territorial, political, economic and cultural power. Peter the Great was succeeded by his widow, Catherine I in 1725, then his cousin, Anna of Courland, who reigned from 1729 to 1740, after which a male Tsar, Ivan VI was proclaimed at two months old. His mother, Anna Leopoldovna, acted as regent for scarcely a year, and in 1741 Peter the Great's daughter (Catherine's mother-in-law) Elizabeth seized the throne.

The marriage between Catherine and Grand Duke Peter was celebrated in 1745, and though there is considerable dispute as to when (and indeed if) it was consummated, Catherine produced an heir, Paul, in 1754. Three years later, she gave birth to a daughter, Anna, who died very young, and who was definitely not Peter's. In April 1762, Catherine had another son – Aleksey – by her lover Grigory Orlov. The boy was given the title of Count Bobrinsky.

The timing of Aleksey's birth is pertinent, in that it may have been a factor in cementing Catherine's plans for a *coup d'état*. The Empress Elizabeth had died in January that year, leaving her nephew Peter as sole Emperor. Peter, a heavy drinker, declared in his cups that he intended to divorce Catherine and marry his mistress. In the last months of her pregnancy, Catherine had to consider her future. The marriage was loveless, without even the polite pretence of respect or fidelity. There were rumours that Peter planned to have her arrested and confined to a monastery, or worse. Threats had been expressed against her children.

Peter possessed some progressive views, but he was broadly unpopular, and in Catherine's opinion unfit to rule. If Catherine wanted to depose him, she would need the support of the Imperial Guard, who in the wake of the Petrine succession laws had become, in a fashion comparable to the Praetorians in Ancient Rome, the queen-makers of Russia. Peter's own political blindness made Catherine's task easier. He had made peace with Frederick of Prussia, Russia's hated opponent in the Seven Years' War, and now planned to march his armies into Denmark (on behalf of his duchy of Holstein), a strategy from which Russia stood to gain no advantage. Furthermore, he was planning to reduce the numbers of the Guards while promoting his Holstein relatives to Russian military commands. To the disgruntled officers, Catherine represented not only a better future for Russia, but for their own interests, too.

In her own words, Catherine saw Peter's fall as inevitable, and her own choice as a blunt necessity: 'it was a matter of either perishing with him (or because of him), or else saving myself, the children, and perhaps the State from the wreckage', she wrote in her memoirs. Whether Catherine indeed plotted the usurpation of her husband as a matter of pragmatic protection, or was motivated by raw ambition, a month after giving birth she was ready to act.

The Emperor was planning to lead his army against Denmark in person, and the scheme was that he should be arrested outside St Petersburg. Catherine could count on a number of loyal officers, who in turn controlled about 10,000 troops. Early on the morning of June 28, 1757, Catherine left the palace of Mon Plaisir to drive to St Petersburg (her hairdresser Michel accompanied her, to arrange her *coiffure* en route). As Catherine visited the barracks of the Guards regiment in turn, the news spread through the city, so that by the time Catherine was making her way to the Winter Palace, she found herself acclaimed by roaring crowds. Dashingly attired in a borrowed uniform of the Preobrazhensky Guards, Catherine reviewed her troops while Peter pursued her to Mon Plaisir. He arrived to find the palace deserted, but only after many hours of drinking and procrastinating did the Emperor appear to grasp the gravity of his position. He finally made his way to the fortress of Kronstadt, from where he intended to launch an advance back into St Petersburg. The garrison received him with the announcement that they, too, had declared for Catherine, and the dejected Emperor, now so drunk he could barely stand, returned to the nearby palace of Oranienbaum. The next day, he abdicated. A week later, he was dead.

Officially the Emperor died of a stroke. In fact he was strangled on the orders of Alexei Orlov, the ambitious brother of Catherine's equally ambitious lover. The extent of Catherine's involvement in Peter's death is unknown – 'the details remain as murky as the deed', but her reputation never recovered from the presumed double crime of mariticide and regicide.

The Ottoman court historian Halil Nuri later described Catherine as 'a vile but fortunate woman'. While the events of the months preceding her coronation in September 1762 were certainly less than glorious, the reign that began when Catherine placed the imperial crown on her own head in the Cathedral of the Assumption in Moscow was, in terms of achievements, magnificent by any reckoning.

Catherine's accession came six years after the Diplomatic Revolution of 1756, which had essentially reconfigured the national alliances that maintained the often uneasy balance of power in Europe. Russia aligned with Austria and France, while Britain, Prussia and Hanover formed a new association. Catherine successfully promulgated the policy of Armed Neutrality, whereby neutral countries could maintain sea trade with belligerent countries, and mediated in the war of the Bavarian Succession, but her main ambitions were the aggrandising of Russia to the south, largely at the expense of the Ottoman Turks, and expansion into Poland. She acquired a vast amount of territory, annexing the Crimea in 1783 and establishing Russian towns and the naval base of Sebastopol on the Black Sea.

While Catherine worked tirelessly at policy and strategy, the one thing she was unable to do, as a woman, was to command her armies, and Russia's military successes were in large part the work of her general Alexander Suvorov and her lover, rumoured husband and lifelong friend Grigori Potemkin. Potemkin was as brilliant as he was excessive, and, in the words of his biographer, the relationship proved an unmatched and 'exuberant political success'.

By refusing to take an official consort, however, Catherine ensured her authority was never diluted. All power ultimately derived from her. As she once remarked to the Swedish ambassador, whatever Potemkin did, it was she who allowed him to do it.

Catherine's reign also inaugurated the period known as the Russian Enlightenment. The Empress was determined that her court should follow her own example in embracing European culture, a policy that was particularly significant for elite women, who had only recently escaped the restrictions of the Muscovite *terem*, according to which well-born women had been secluded in separate living quarters, made to wear concealing clothing and travel in closed carriages – in short, excluded from participation in society. Released from obligatory service to the Imperial Court and enjoying newfound social freedoms, the Russian nobility welcomed a cultural renaissance. Catherine herself was the model – she composed music, wrote plays, corresponded with the leading figures of the

Enlightenment, including Voltaire, patronized opera and ballet and amassed the enormous art collection that became the basis of the holdings of the Hermitage Museum. She founded the Smolny Institute for the education of aristocratic young women, the first of its type in Russia, and attempted, though with limited success, to inaugurate a free national system of primary and secondary education for all. Ferociously hardworking and endlessly curious, Catherine's *Memoirs* and her vast correspondence provide enough incident for half a dozen lives.

'A pretty fair summary', said Catherine, 'But you've left out most of the lovers.'

Certainly, Catherine's private life has blazed down the centuries as brightly as the avenues of burning firs and cypress trees that once lit her sleighs as she travelled across the northern steppe. Her propensity for younger beauties was supposedly her great weakness – as Byron put it in *Don Juan*, 'for though she would widow all/Nations, she liked man as an individual'.

('Him again', said Lucrezia. 'Nasty little man.')

Catherine was generous to her gentlemen – however, the story that she first had them tried by an 'eprouveuse', her friend and later rival Countess Praskovya Bruce, is as apocryphal as the existence of her notorious 'erotic cabinet'. The post of official lover was not dissimilar to that of the *'maitresse en titre'*, which had been enjoyed by the kings of France and England for centuries, though Catherine had the excellent sense to maintain them as no more than personal companions with no political influence whatsoever. This avoided (despite the men's and the court's best efforts) the possibility of factions forming around them. Catherine's contemporaries were nevertheless both appalled and titillated by the openness with which she conducted her sex life, and determined to see her private affairs as influencing her policies.

'Frederick of Prussia said "It is a terrible business when the prick and the cunt decide the interest of Europe"', put in Catherine.

'Must you be so vulgar?' said Lucrezia.

I lowered my papers. 'That's the problem for all of you, really. Sex. All the accounts are obsessed with it. Look here – Diderot on you, Catherine: "The soul of Caesar with the seductions of Cleopatra".'

'What would he know?' said Cleopatra indignantly.

'So what?' said Catherine 'I liked handsome young men. There has to be some compensation for working every hour God sends for thirty-five years, and besides, there was only a dozen or so. No one gives Louis XV a hard time. And it was practical ... most of the time.'

'True. But still, they can't shut up about it. As for you ...' I rifled among my notes, turning to Cleopatra. 'Here we are. If I may?'

FIVE

Leaving the City

Sensual excess perfumes Cleopatra's story down the ages. Horace lauded her defeat as a consequence of her supposed drunkenness:

> Great Caesar taught her dizzy brain,
> Made mad by Mareotic grape,
> To feel the sobering truth of pain.

Propertius warned of the helplessness to which her sexual powers reduced men; to Boccaccio, she was 'the whore of Eastern kings'. Dante confines her to the second circle of hell, among the *'peccator carnali'*, the carnal sinners who have fallen prey to lust, and Virgil painted her as the 'shameless Egyptian consort' on Aeneas's shield. Plutarch warily sang her enchanting attractions, while Lucan saw her extravagance and ambition in terms of sexual domination – her beauty, like Helen of Troy's, being responsible for a civil war. Visually, Michelangelo (in a drawing later painted by Vasari), associated the coils of her twining hair with the Medusa's snakes, the fatal asp nestling in Cleopatra's locks like a fashionable ornament. Guido Reni and Guerino placed it tauntingly close to her naked breast, while Artemisia Gentileschi depicted her unclothed at the moment of suicide. In short, Cleopatra became a catch-all trope for the erotic.

In Christine's *Book of the City of Ladies*, ferocity is no barrier to entry. Among other examples, she cites the case of Berenice of Cappadoccia, who, when her brother-in-law rebelled against her regency, confronted him in battle, killed him with her own hands and drove her chariot triumphantly over his body.

'She doesn't even mind about the incest', said Lucrezia, turning a page in my copy. 'Look: Semiramis, the queen of Nineveh and conqueror of Babylon, married her own son. And why? "She wanted no other crowned lady to share her empire"'.

'And because she thought no man other than her son was worthy of her', said Cleopatra, craning over Lucrezia's shoulder.

'Christine excuses Semiramis because she was a heathen', I pointed out. 'She didn't know any better.'

'So am I, come to that', said Cleopatra. 'It was Caesar who insisted on putting up that gaudy statue. Stubbornness, that was his problem. Christine agrees that he'd never have been assassinated if only he'd listened to his wife.'

'Voltaire called me the Semiramis of the North', said Catherine, hopefully.

In history, it seems that powerful women can never escape their own corporeality. Whether women are being castigated or lauded, historical practice casts them biologically as other, as exceptional for good or bad, in a manner to which men are simply not subject. Maleness is seen neither as an obstacle to be explained away, nor as an automatic negative. Power in males is not aberrant; it is accepted, taken for granted. When mighty women are judged politically, opposition frequently elides into moral, *ergo* sexual disapproval. However rousing Christine is on the subject of Eve, she does not doubt that sex is the original sin and women the original sinners. Sexual continence is the only way to guarantee entry into the city:

> My ladies, see how these men assail you on all sides and accuse you of every vice imaginable ... refute the criticisms they make of you by behaving morally ... Drive back these treacherous liars who use nothing but tricks and honeyed words to steal from you that which you should keep safe above all else: your chastity.

Commenting on Catherine's reign, the eighteenth-century Ottoman diplomat Ahmed Vasif contrasts the idea of *adl*, the personal or political rightness of something that occupies its proper place, with *zulm*, 'putting a thing in a place not its own', with implications of moral transgression. To Ottoman historians, Catherine was an object of fascination and hostility not because she was a woman per se, but because she was a powerful woman. She was *zulm*. Things which are in their proper places require no qualification, hence it remains the case that men are writers and rulers; women are women writers and women rulers. Critically, then, Christine, Catherine, Cleopatra and Lucrezia are in the same historical position, unable to be understood beyond the context of their femaleness.

The legacies of Lucrezia Borgia, Catherine the Great and Cleopatra the Last are historically subsumed by fraught representations of sexuality. In Cleopatra's case, her defeat at Actium was interpreted as the restoration of a natural order, both sexually and politically, whereby the Roman virtues embodied in Octavian ultimately ended both the Ptolemaic dynasty and the Roman civil wars. 'Validity was restored to the laws, authority to the courts and dignity to the Senate', claimed Velleius. Cleopatra became a propaganda pin-up: insatiable, treacherous, power-drunk, bloodthirsty, the defeated counterpoint to the Roman state. As the face of a whole culture, Cleopatra's submission at Actium represented the fulcrum of a new era, one in which Octavian brilliantly represented the arrogation of power to his person as a return to the mores of the Republic. His distortion of the principles and practice of Roman government coalesce in the eager contrasts of Cleopatra with the prudence and dignity of Roman matrons such as Octavia, whose values her brother appropriated even as his imperial ambitions undermined them. He was a tyrant who disguised his own tyranny by celebrating his defeat of Cleopatra's.

Lucrezia's reputation connects with Cleopatra's especially neatly through representations of both women in the late fifteenth and sixteenth centuries, a period notable both for its abundance of female rulers

(Catherine de Medici, Mary Tudor, Elizabeth I, Margaret of Austria, Isabella of Castile and others), and the wealth of criticism contesting their rule. Cleopatra figures in *de casibus* tragedy (a popular genre of Renaissance theatre centred on exemplary fallen rulers), most prominently perhaps, to the Anglo-Saxon mind, in Shakespeare. There is also Aemilia Lanyer's *Salve Deus Rex Judaeorum* (1611), and, in France, Etienne Jodelle's *Cléopâtre captive* (1552). In these plays Cleopatra is portrayed as both vauntingly ambitious and reassuringly submissive. Her suicide – once the threat she represented is passed – can be celebrated as brave and honourable, with the Renaissance taking its cue from Horace's *Nunc est bibendum*:

> That she, no vulgar dame should grace,
> A triumph, crownless and a slave.

In Renaissance retellings, the restoration of order to Rome is thus translated into the necessity for women to bow to male authority, as in

Boccaccio's *De claris mulieribus* (*Concerning Famous Women*), from 1374. For him, Cleopatra's erotic potency was both titillating and reassuring: even as it taunts and tantalizes, Cleopatra's naked body provided a glimpse of rapturous pagan sin safely prismed through Christian political virtue. Similarly, Jacob Burckhardt, the canonical Renaissance critic, saw Lucrezia as 'the icon of the negative heroine', whose fame is based not on virtue but rather, on 'promiscuity, manipulation and murder'. (Perhaps unsurprisingly, Lucrezia's mother, Vannozza dei Cattanei, didn't see it that way. Her epitaph in Santa Maria del Popolo in Rome, was inscribed: 'mother of ... Lucrezia of Ferrara, ennobled by her children'. Vannozza chose to celebrate Lucrezia as a vindication of her own life, yet the epitaph was removed in 1568, during the particularly strict papacy of Pius V. Vannozza's pride, then, remained invisible until the monument was rediscovered in 1947.)

On Catherine's death, meanwhile, her son Paul ended the age of Empresses by legislating to re-establish male primogeniture in the Romanov dynasty. In short, whatever their genuine achievements may have been, these women are still judged by history (including feminist history) on the assumption that their positions were anomalous. They are not seen, beyond category, as extraordinary individuals, but rather constantly measured against the paradigm of femininity.

'So what are you going to do about it?'

'Me?' I asked 'What *can* I do about it? I'm just a poor and ignorant scholar, here in my gloomy retreat.'

'It is a bit dingy in here', remarked Catherine. 'if you don't mind me saying. You could do with a bit of gold leaf. Or maybe marble ...'

'I'm also asleep', I said firmly.

'It's true though', said Cleopatra. 'It's all about the body. What was it they said about my nose: "had it been shorter, the whole aspect of the world would have been altered"? Who was that again?'

'Pascal', said Catherine. 'I read all his work.'

'You might say the same thing about Napoleon's cock', said Lucrezia. 'What would the world have looked like had that been an inch longer? No one seems to ask that.'

'Who's being vulgar now?', said Catherine. ('Good point though.')

What would history look like if its male protagonists were understood and judged in line with their sex lives, if the political decisions of Charles V or Louis XIV or Abraham Lincoln were read through the prism of gender? The idea seems ridiculous (not to mention boring). The corollary to 'Well-Behaved Women' persists, however. 'Badly Behaved Women' do still seem to be the ones making history. Yet as Jane Marcus asked in 2008, in a review of Ulrich's *Well-Behaved Women Seldom Make History*, 'does notoriety still ensure ignominy and social ostracism in those women's lives, and then, perhaps, posthumous honour by historians?' That 'honour' is still constructed around their status as women.

Enormous quantities of ink have been expended in discussing the relationship between power and the female body. Equally, the very definition of the 'female' body – who is or is not a woman; where 'femininity' resides – remains the object of passionate contemporary debate. Christine de Pisan, who framed her arguments within the Christian context of her period, cut through the conundrum by emphasizing the human qualities of her subjects. In her discussion with Reason, Christine quotes Cicero's argument that men should not be subject to women because of women's biological inferiority. Reason replies: 'It is he or she who is the more virtuous that is the superior being: human superiority or inferiority is not determined by sexual difference but by the degree to which one has perfected one's nature and morals'.

The point, Christine argues, is not whether one is male or female, but rather that one is possessed of rationality and a soul. In a snappy reprisal of Genesis, Christine reminds her readers that not only was the Divine Craftsman not ashamed to create the female form, 'there are some who are foolish enough to maintain that when God made man in His image, this means his physical body'. Since Jesus Christ had not been born when Adam and Eve lived in Paradise, God *had* no human form. 'His image' must, then, be understood to refer to the soul, with which he endowed both male and female equally. In Christine's view, gender is irrelevant to virtue.

'But sex itself most definitely is relevant', said Catherine. 'So I don't see how any of this helps us.'

Sexual difference, like race or class, is obviously hugely relevant to understanding history. But perhaps we should beware of a 'Whig' version of feminist history into which historical women are neatly inserted as struts of a progressive ladder that ascends inevitably towards empowerment. It may be a positive trajectory, but it remains a reductive one.

'You weren't feminists', I said slowly. 'It's not

useful to claim that. Any more than that you were wicked.'

'But Christine would never have thought we were *respectable*. As you said, she's quite specific about scandalous behaviour.'

'Are you sure you want to live in Christine's city anyway?' I asked. 'A city of ladies could get dull. Especially for you Catherine. Not to mention the upkeep on such an old structure ...'

'Don't', said Catherine to Lucrezia.

At the conclusion of *The Book of the City of Ladies*, Christine quotes the figure of Reason: 'I prophesy that this city ... will never fall or be taken ... Though it may be attacked on all sides, it will never be defeated'.

Maybe though, it is time to dismantle the walls. Reason might also suggest that reducing historical women to 'good' or 'bad', whether pioneers or victims, is to diminish them. Cordoning them off in compendiums of their own, no matter how apparently empowering, seems not all that different to the segregation of Russia's pre-eighteenth-century *terem* (credit for the abolishment of which must, incidentally, go not to Catherine, but to her grandfather-in-law, Peter the Great). Not only does the manner in which women are perceived in popular history communicate broader attitudes to authority, sexuality and emancipation, it also depends on 'women' as a static category, or rather on 'female' being opposed to 'male'. Remove the category, as Christine removed the physical body, and you dissolve the distinction between virtue and vice as it pertains biologically.

At the conclusion of *City*, Justice bids Christine farewell, and Christine, having been convinced by the arguments of the three allegories, is free to address her readers in her own voice. She does not extend her use of the dream vision into a fictional 'awakening'. It has served its purpose. Dream-visions are not the same as dreams, in that while they can bend the rules of time and space, allowing 'the marvellous into the everyday', they are a disciplined literary device, not a journey into the unconscious.

They are re-tellings of the possible, a means of reflecting on reality.

Yet fantasies are truths about our internal lives. For Christine, the dream-vision was a means of radically addressing the work of the generations of scholars who preceded her, in order to correct their dismissal of the equality of women's souls. In reconsidering the possible from a contemporary perspective, it might be that my visitors were right. Can 'woman' as a category be retired from historical practice? Paradoxically, one way to write certain women back into history might be not to write them as women at all.

Acknowledgements

Many thanks to Toby Mundy. Thea Lenarduzzi and Roz Dineen have been the most sensitive and sympathetic of editors, it has been a great pleasure to work together on this. Thanks too to Owen Matthews for fascinating observations on powerful women.

Notes

5 'the first time that we see a woman' Simone de Beauvoir, *The Second Sex* (trans. and ed.) H.M. Parshley (New York: Knopf, 1953), p. 128

17 'never to her lover truer queen' Geoffrey Chaucer, *The Legend of Good Women*, lines 496–7

20 'A deadly powder mixed with sugar' Paolo Giovio cited in Rachel Erlanger, *Lucrezia Borgia* (London: Hawthorn, 1977), p. 227

22 'well-behaved woman' Quoted in Jane Marcus review of Laurel Ulrich, *Well-Behaved Women Seldom Make History* that appeared in *Tulsa Studies in Women's Literature*, Vol. 27, No. 1 (Spring 2008)

23 'black legends' Robert Knecht, 'Catherine
de Medici: Saint or Sinner?' *History Review*,
No. 26 (December 1996)

34 'the occult, alchemical East' Stacy Schiff,
'Rehabilitating Cleopatra', *Smithsonian
Magazine*, December 2010

34 'Cleopatra's close identification with Antony'
Toby Wilkinson, *The Rise and Fall of Ancient
Egypt* (London: Bloomsbury, 2010), p. 506

36 'For notwithstanding all the appearance of
Fondness' Sarah Fielding, *The Lives of
Cleopatra and Octavia* (London, 1757),
p. 64

39 'the greatest whore that ever was in Rome'
Francesco Matarazzo, 'Cronaca dell Citta di
Perugia dal 1492 al 1503', *Archivio Storico
Italiano*, Vol. XVI

41 'her mouth is rather large' Bernardino
Zambotti, *Diario Ferrarese* cited in Anny
Latour, *The Borgias* (London: Elek, 1963),
p. 130

43 'there were reports that not only did the
brothers' Francesco Guicciardini, *Storia*

d'Italia (ed.) C. Groppetti (Novara: Interlinea, 2019), p. 796

46 'Madonna Lucrezia, who is wise' *Atti e memorie della Deputazione veneta di Storia patria* cited in Latour, ibid., p. 84

46 'Every day people are found murdered' Marin Sanudo, *La Spedizione di Carlo VIII in Italia* (Venice, 1873), Chapter VIII

48 'Before His Holiness ... left Rome' Johannes Burchard, *Diarium* (ed.) L. Thuasne (3 vols) Paris: Liber Notarum, 1885)

54 'a prerogative claimed by no other contemporary monarch' Anthony Lentin cited in Russell E. Martin, *Law, Succession, and the Eighteenth-Century Refounding of the Romanov Dynasty* https://static1. squarespace.com/static/55db620de4b 06d457a3de880/t/565b465de4b05e0c71c 747e6/1448822365975/18_RMartin_225-42. pdf

57 'it was a matter of either perishing' see Simon Sebag Montefiore, *Catherine the Great and Potemkin: The Imperial Love Affair*

(London: Weidenfeld and Nicolson, 2016), pp. 47–9

59 'the details remain as murky as the deed' Ibid., p. 58

59 'a vile but fortunate woman' Ethan L. Menchinger, 'Contemporary Ottoman Views of Catherine the Great', *Journal for Eighteenth-Century Studies* (October 2018)

62 'for though she would widow all' George Gordon Byron, *Don Juan*, Canto IX Verse 63

65 'Great Caesar taught her dizzy brain' Translations of Horace are from John Corrington's bouncy 1882 translation

69 'putting a thing in a place not its own' Menchinger, ibid.

74 'does notoriety still ensure ignominy' Marcus, ibid., p. 164

78 'the marvellous into the everyday' E. V. Gordon (ed.), *Pearl* (Oxford: Oxford University Press, 1986), p. xiv

Bibliography

De Pisan, Christine, *The Book of the City of Ladies* (ed.) Rosalind Brown-Grant (London: Penguin, 1999)

De Pisan, Christine, *Le Livre de l'advision de Cristine* (eds) Christine Reno and Liliane Dulac (Paris: Honore Champion, 2004)

Journals

Behuniak Long, Susan, 'The Significance of Lucrezia in Machiavelli's *La Mandragola*', *Review of Politics*, Vol. 51 (Spring 1989)

Blumenfeld-Kosinski, Renate, 'Christine de Pizan and the Misogynistic Tradition', *Romantic Review*, No. 81 (1990)

Curtius, L. *Ikonographische Beitrage zum Portrait der romischen Republic und der julisch-calusdischen Familie*: *RM*, No. 48 (1933)

Diamond, Arlyn, Comment on Sheila Delany's 'Review of "The Order of the Rose: The Life and Times of Christine de Pisan"', *Signs*, Vol. 4 (Spring 1979)

Marcus, Jane, review of *Well-Behaved Women Seldom Make History* by Laurel Thatcher Ulrich, from *Tulsa Studies in Women's Literature*, Vol. 27, No. 1 (Spring 2008)

Menchinger, Ethan L., 'Contemporary Ottoman Views of Catherine the Great', *Journal for Eighteenth-Century Studies* (October 2018)

Paglia, Camille, 'Feminism Past and Present: Ideology, Action and Reform', *Arion: A Journal of Humanities and the Classics*, Third Series, Vol. 6, No. 1 (Spring/Summer 2008)

Reinhold, Meyer, 'The Declaration of War Against Cleopatra', *Classical Journal*, Vol. 77, No. 2 (December 1981)

Rigby, Stephen H., 'The Body Politic in the Social and Political Thought of Christine de Pizan', *Cahiers de Recherches Médiévales et Humanistes*, No. 24 (2012)

Rudy, Kathryn M., 'An Illustrated Mid-Fifteenth-Century Primer for a Flemish Girl: British Library, Harley MS 3828', *Journal of the Warburg and Courtauld Institutes*, Vol. 69 (2006)

Skeat, T.C., 'The Last Days of Cleopatra: A Chronological Problem', *Journal of Roman Studies*, Vol. 43 (1953)

Volumes

Delogu, Daisy, *Allegorical Bodies: Power and Gender in Late Medieval France* (Toronto: University of Toronto Press, 2015)

Erlanger, Rachel, *Lucrezia Borgia* (London: Hawthorn, 1977)

Fielding, Sarah, *The Lives of Cleopatra and Octavia* (London, 1757)

Figes, Orlando, *Natasha's Dance: A Cultural History of Russia* (London: Allen Lane, 2002)

Gordon, E. V. (ed.), *Pearl* (Oxford: Oxford University Press, 1986)

Guicciardini, Francesco, *Storia d'Italia* (ed.) C. Groppetti (Novara: Interlinea, 2019)

Irvine, Martin, *The Making of Textual Culture: Grammatica and Literary Theory 350–1100* (Cambridge: Cambridge University Press, 1994)

Latour, Anny, *The Borgias* (London: Elek, 1963)

Lodi, Letizia and Lisa Hilton, *La Morte de Cleopatra* (Milan: Skira, 2016)

Maroger, D. (ed.) *Catherine the Great: Memoirs* (London, 1955)

Moneera Laennec, Christine, 'Christine Antygrafe: Authorial Ambivalence in the Work of Christine de Pisan' in Carol J. Singley and Susan Elizabeth Sweeney (eds), *Anxious Power: Reading, Writing and Ambivalence in Narrative by Women* (New

York: State University of New York Press, 1993)

Pelner Cosman, Madeleine and Linda G. Jones (eds), *Handbook to Life in the Medieval World* (New York: Infobase Press, 2008)

Sebag Montefiore, Simon, *Catherine the Great and Potemkin: The Imperial Love Affair* (London: Weidenfeld and Nicolson, 2016)

Strathern, Paul, *The Borgias* (London: Atlantic, 2019)

Turner, Victor, *The Anthropology of Performance* (New York: PAJ Publications, 1987)

Wilkinson, Toby, *The Rise and Fall of Ancient Egypt: The History of a Civilisation from 3000 BC to Cleopatra* (London: Bloomsbury, 2010)

Zarri, Gabriella, *La Religione di Lucrezia Borgia* (Rome: Edizioni Roma nel Rinascimento, 2006)

TLS

Enjoyed the book?

Subscribe today

Discuss, decipher and delve into the world around you with a *TLS* subscription. An archive going back to 1902; ideas updated every week.

- The print edition, delivered weekly
- Unrestricted access to the *TLS* website & App
- Full use of the *TLS* Archive going back to 1902
- Exclusive reads and online-only features
- A first look at the *TLS* with the weekly newsletter

Subscribe to the *TLS* today for just £1 a week for 6 weeks.

Go to the-tls.co.uk/HILTON to subscribe today.

Also from TLS Books

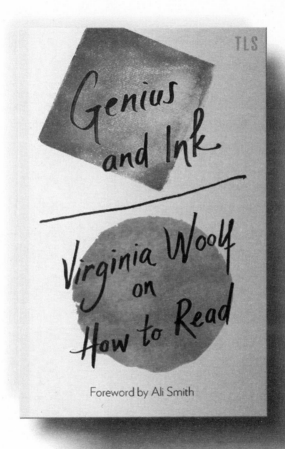

Who better to serve as a guide to great books and their authors than Virginia Woolf?

Also from TLS Books

The bestselling author of the Jack Reacher books explores what makes a hero